D1533713

Copyright © 1980, 2005 by Lemniscaat b.v. Rotterdam
Originally published in the Netherlands under the title
Er ligt een krokodil onder mijn bed!
All rights reserved
Printed in Belgium
Second U.S. edition, 2005
Second printing

LIBRARY OF CONGRESS CATALOGING-IN-PUBLICATION DATA
Schubert, Ingrid.
[Er ligt een krokodil onder mijn bed!. English]
There's a crocodile under my bed! / Ingrid and Dieter Schubert.—2nd U.S. ed.
1 v. : col. Ill. ; 27 cm.
Originally published under the title *Er ligt een krokodil onder mijn bed!*: Rotterdam, Netherlands : Lemniscaat.
Summary: Peggy enjoys a night of playing with the not-at-all-frightening crocodile she finds under her bed.
ISBN-13: 978-1-932425-48-2
ISBN-10: 1-932425-48-9 (alk. paper)
[1. Crocodiles—Fiction. 2. Bedtime—Fiction.] I. Schubert, Dieter. II. Title.
PZ7.S3834 Th 2005
[E]—dc22
2005019093

LEMNISCAAT
An Imprint of Boyds Mills Press, Inc.
A Highlights Company
815 Church Street
Honesdale, Pennsylvania 18431

hubert, Ingrid, 1953–
ere's a crocodile
der my bed! /
05.
305227572884
            03/13/13

There's a Crocodile Under My Bed!

Ingrid and Dieter Schubert

Lemniscaat
Asheville, North Carolina

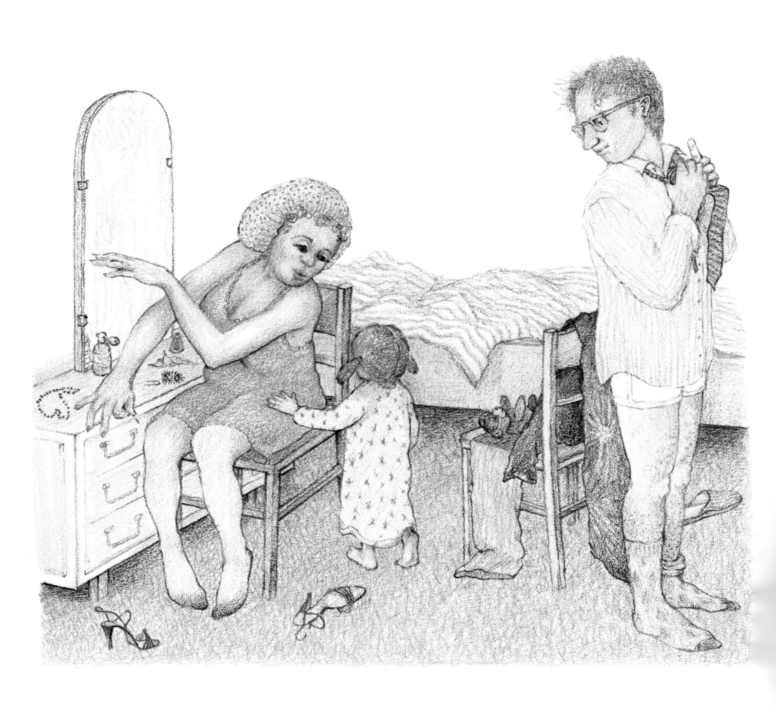

"Time for bed, Peggy," says Dad.
Mom and Dad are going out, so
there's no time for a story tonight.

Peggy skips along the corridor to her room, opens
the door, and ... Oh! There is a crocodile hiding
under her bed, his eyes shining yellow in the dark.

"I can't go to sleep!" Peggy yells to her parents. "There's a crocodile under my bed!"

"Oh, Peggy," Mom says, sighing. "We haven't got time for games now."

"Show me," says Dad. He switches on the light in her room, and they look under the bed.

"No crocodile," says Dad. "Just shoes and toys and a lot of old rubbish. Now go to sleep, Peggy. Grandma's here, but don't call her unless you have to."

He tucks her in, turns out the light, and leaves the room.

Peggy hears someone giggling. She looks under the bed—no one is there.

"Up here!"

A huge crocodile is grinning at Peggy from the top of the wardrobe.

"I'm Henry," he says, jumping down.

Peggy says nothing. She just clutches her bear and stares, round-eyed.

"You're not scared, are you?" says
Henry. "I'm very friendly." He begins
to shrink, getting smaller and smaller
until he could fit into Peggy's shoe. "Do
you like me better this size?" he asks.

Peggy thinks for a minute, then
smiles at him. "I prefer you big," she
says, "so we can play with each other."

In a few seconds, Henry is his normal
size again.

"What shall we play first?" asks Peggy.

But Henry is covered with dust from the top of the
wardrobe. "I would like to wash first," he says.

So Peggy runs a bath, with lots of Mom's bubble bath,
and Henry jumps in. "Come and join me," he cries.
"It's lovely and warm."

Peggy is a sea monster, threatening the boats and tipping the dolls into the water.

Henry rescues them with his tail, swishing them over the side to safety.

The water is getting cold. Peggy shows Henry how long she can hold her breath under water. Then they dry themselves and go downstairs.

"Let's have some music," says Henry. "I will teach you the Crocodile Rock."

Peggy turns on the radio, and away they go. The Crocodile Rock is great! They dance until they have no breath left.

"You're the best crocodile dancer ever," says Peggy, panting.

"Now what shall we do?"
asks Peggy.
  "Let's make a crocodile,"
says Henry. "A tiny one."

"We need two egg cartons," says Henry, "one bigger than the other, if possible. We need green paint and red paint and paint brushes. We need white paper and scissors and glue and a piece of string."

They glue the big egg carton so it stays shut. That makes the body. They paint the small egg carton red inside and stick in sharp pointy teeth cut out of white paper. That makes the head. They attach a paper tail to one end of the body and tie the head to the other. Then they paint the crocodile green outside with two fierce eyes.

"He looks much more frightening than you, Henry," giggles Peggy.

Peggy is beginning to yawn, so Henry carries her to bed.

"I'll tell you a story," he says, "about me when I was little. I lived in the Land of Crocodiles, which is sunny and beautiful and far away. Many animals lived there—elephants and ostriches and hippopotamuses and tortoises and, of course, crocodiles.

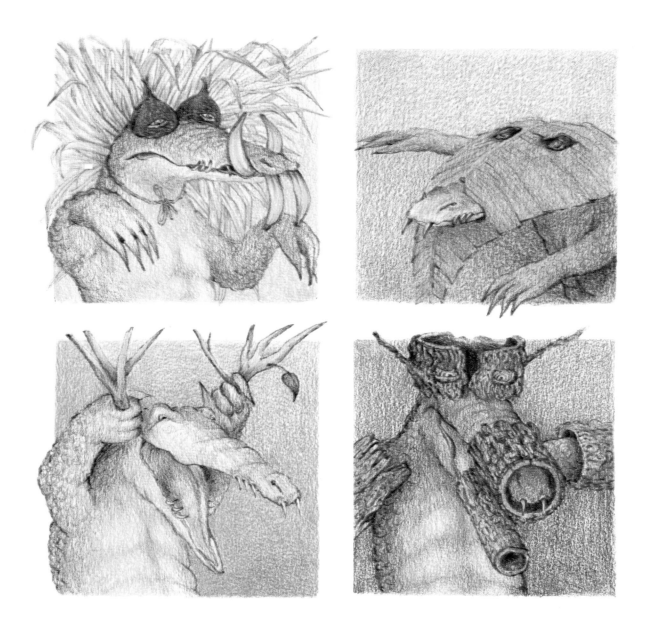

"I was very naughty, and I used to tease the small animals. I told them scary stories about ghosts and witches. I dressed up as a monster to frighten them. Once I rose out of the river with long seaweed hair, and they all ran away.

"Then I had a very wicked idea. I swapped the ostrich eggs with the crocodile eggs. When the babies hatched out, their parents were furious.

"The babies of the crocodiles had feathers and beaks. The babies of the ostriches had scaly skins and wanted to swim in the river.

"I was in terrible trouble.

"I was called before the Council of Seven Wise Crocodiles. The eldest of the Wise Crocodiles told me what they had decided to do.

"'You have behaved very badly,' he said. 'You have scared the small animals and upset their parents. This must stop. We are sending you away to the Land of Men. Many children there are afraid—of the dark, perhaps, or of bad dreams. You must learn to comfort them and teach them that there is nothing to fear. Will you try?'

"I promised I would.

"'To help you, we will give you two gifts,' he said. 'You will be able to speak the language of men, and you will be able to make yourself tiny so as not to scare anyone. When you have visited a thousand children, you can come back to the Land of Crocodiles.'

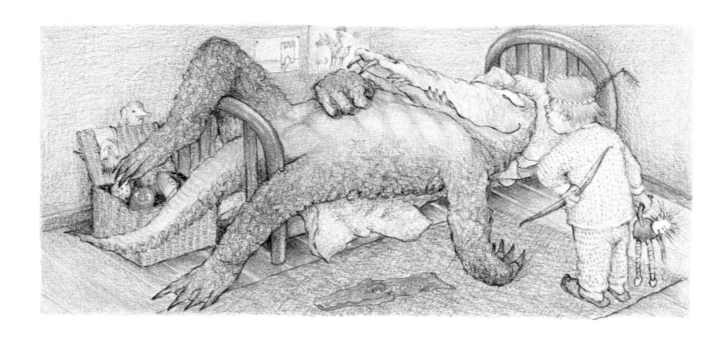

"The Wise Crocodiles gave me a drink that sent me to
sleep, and when I woke up I was in a little boy's room—
in fact, I was lying in his bed! We had great fun playing
Cowboys and Indians together.

"You, Peggy, are the seven hundred and seventy-sixth child
I have visited. One day ..." Henry stops, for Peggy is asleep.

He gently tucks her in, turns out the light, and leaves the room.

"Hello, Peggy," says Mum next
morning. She opens the curtains,
letting in bright sunshine.

"Look," says Dad, laughing. "There
was a crocodile under your bed, Peggy.
An egg-carton crocodile!"

Peggy just smiles.